Dear Parents:

Congratulations! Your child is taking the first steps on an exciting journey. The destination? Independent reading!

STEP INTO READING® will help your child get there. The program offers five steps to reading success. Each step includes fun stories and colorful art or photographs. In addition to original fiction and books with favorite characters, there are Step into Reading Non-Fiction Readers, Phonics Readers and Boxed Sets, Sticker Readers, and Comic Readers—a complete literacy program with something to interest every child.

Learning to Read, Step by Step!

Ready to Read   Preschool–Kindergarten
• big type and easy words • rhyme and rhythm • picture clues
For children who know the alphabet and are eager to begin reading.

Reading with Help   Preschool–Grade 1
• basic vocabulary • short sentences • simple stories
For children who recognize familiar words and sound out new words with help.

Reading on Your Own   Grades 1–3
• engaging characters • easy-to-follow plots • popular topics
For children who are ready to read on their own.

Reading Paragraphs   Grades 2–3
• challenging vocabulary • short paragraphs • exciting stories
For newly independent readers who read simple sentences with confidence.

Ready for Chapters   Grades 2–4
• chapters • longer paragraphs • full-color art
For children who want to take the plunge into chapter books but still like colorful pictures.

STEP INTO READING® is designed to give every child a successful reading experience. The grade levels are only guides; children will progress through the steps at their own speed, developing confidence in their reading.

Remember, a lifetime love of reading starts with a single step!

Copyright © 2025 Disney Enterprises, Inc. and Pixar. All rights reserved. Published in the United States by Random House Children's Books, a division of Penguin Random House LLC, 1745 Broadway, New York, NY 10019, and in Canada by Penguin Random House Canada Limited, Toronto, in conjunction with Disney Enterprises, Inc.

Step Into Reading, Random House, and the Random House colophon are registered trademarks of Penguin Random House LLC.

Visit us on the Web!
StepIntoReading.com
rhcbooks.com

ISBN 978-0-7364-4424-8 (trade) — ISBN 978-0-7364-9043-6 (lib.bdg.)
ISBN 978-0-7364-4425-5 (ebook)

Printed in the United States of America

10 9 8 7 6 5 4 3 2 1

Random House Children's Books supports the First Amendment and celebrates the right to read.

STEP INTO READING
Step 3

Elio's New Friends

adapted by Kristine Osaki
illustrated by the Disney Storybook Art Team

Random House 🏠 New York

Elio Solís

Eleven-year-old Elio Solís
has a big imagination
and even bigger dreams.
More than anything,
he wants aliens to take him
to outer space.
Elio's dream is unusual
compared to other kids',
but he does not mind
being different from
everyone else.

Rain or shine, Elio goes to the beach every day to look for aliens.
He wears a costume and makes a big sign so that aliens can see him.

He also listens to the radio
to find secret alien messages.
He does not care how long
he might have to wait.
He cannot miss a chance
to go to space.

Olga Solís

Olga Solís is Elio's aunt.
She is a successful major
in the Air Force.
Her biggest challenge is not
her job—it is taking care
of her nephew, Elio!
She does not understand
his obsession with space and
wishes he would make friends
and stay out of trouble.

Gunther Melmac

Gunther Melmac works for Olga. He is passionate about his job and spends all his time thinking about space and aliens. He believes he has located a message that was sent to Earth by aliens.

Elio finds out about Melmac's discovery. This proves that aliens are real! He prepares for their arrival.

But Olga is frustrated.

She wants Elio to forget aliens and go to summer camp.

Elio does not want to go to camp.

Bryce and Caleb

Elio meets Bryce and Caleb at the beach. They get into an argument, and Elio's eye is hurt. The three boys are sent to summer camp as punishment. Bryce and Caleb blame Elio and continue to bother him.

Later that night, something
incredible happens.
A beam of light pulls Elio
into the sky toward a spaceship!
Elio cannot believe
this is happening.
His dream is coming true!

Ooooo

The spaceship brings Elio to a bright white room. Elio meets a supercomputer named Ooooo.

Ooooo is ready to assist Elio and will take him to meet the alien leaders.

Elio arrives in a space city known as the Communiverse. Aliens from multiple galaxies gather in the Communiverse to share ideas and work together. The aliens think Elio is the leader of Earth.

Questa

Elio meets an alien named Questa.
She floats in the air
and can read minds!
Questa is kind and always sees
the best in everyone.

Helix

Helix is smart and a bit stuffy. He knows everything about the Communiverse. He is excited to welcome Elio as a new member.

Other Elio

While Elio is in the Communiverse, someone needs to take his place at home. Ooooo uses cloning clay

to create an exact copy of Elio!
Other Elio will pretend to be
Elio on Earth.
They send Other Elio
through a portal.

Lord Grigon

Elio learns that not all aliens are friendly. Lord Grigon is a warrior

who wants to destroy
the Communiverse.
To make peace,
Elio talks to Lord Grigon.

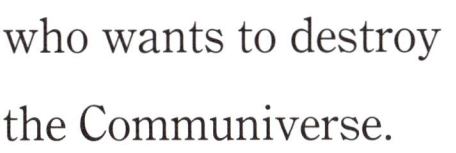

Glordon

While Elio is on Grigon's ship,

he meets Grigon's son, Glordon.

At first Elio is scared,

but Glordon is a kid, too!

He swaddles Elio in a web
to help him feel safe.
Glordon is excited to meet
another kid like him.

Elio and Glordon go to the Communiverse together. They have fun exploring and trying new things.

Neither Elio nor Glordon has had a true friend before. This means that they are now best friends.

In the Communiverse,
Elio finds adventure, friendship,
and a galaxy of possibility.
But living in space is not
as easy as Elio thought.
He knows his home will always
be on Earth with his aunt Olga.